A Sheltered Woman

Also by Yiyun Li

Gold Boy, Emerald Girl
The Vagrants
A Thousand Years of Good Prayers
Kinder Than Solitude

A Sheltered Woman

Woman

Yiyun Li

FOURTH ESTATE • *London*

Fourth Estate
An imprint of HarperCollins*Publishers*
1 London Bridge Street
London SE1 9GF
www.4thestate.co.uk

First published in Great Britain in 2015 by Fourth Estate
First published in the United States in 2014 by *The New Yorker*

A catalogue record for this book is
available from the British Library

ISBN 978-0-00-815367-0

Printed and bound in Spain by
Rodesa, S.L., Villatuerta

MIX
Paper from
responsible sources
FSC C007454

A Sheltered Woman

A Sheltered Woman

The new mother, groggy from a nap, sat at the table as though she did not grasp why she had been summoned. Perhaps she never would, Auntie Mei thought. On the place mat sat a bowl of soybean-and-pig's-foot soup that Auntie Mei had cooked, as she had for many new mothers before this one. Many, however, was not exact. In her interviews with potential employers, Auntie Mei always gave the precise number of families she had worked for: 126 when she interviewed with her current employer, 131 babies altogether. The families' contact information, the dates she had worked for them, their babies' names and birthdays – these she had recorded in a palm-size notebook, which had twice fallen apart and been taped back together. Years ago, Auntie Mei had bought it at a garage sale in Moline, Illinois. She had liked the picture of flowers on the cover, purple and yellow, unmelted snow surrounding the chaste petals. She had liked the price of the notebook, too: five cents. When she handed a dime to the child with the cash box on his lap, she asked if there was another notebook she could buy, so that he would not have to give her any change; the boy looked perplexed and said no. It was greed that had made her ask, but when the memory came back – it often did when she took the notebook out of her suitcase for another interview – Auntie Mei would laugh at herself: why on earth had she wanted two notebooks, when there's not enough life to fill one?

The mother sat still, not touching the spoon, until teardrops fell into the steaming soup.

'Now, now,' Auntie Mei said. She was pushing herself and the baby in a new rocking chair – back and forth, back and forth, the squeaking less noticeable than yesterday. I wonder who's enjoying the rocking more, she said to herself: the chair, whose job is to rock until it breaks apart, or you, whose life is being rocked away? And which one of you will meet your demise first? Auntie Mei had long ago accepted that she had, despite her best intentions, become one of those people who talk to themselves when the world is not listening. At least she took care not to let the words slip out.

'I don't like this soup,' said the mother, who surely had a Chinese name but had asked Auntie Mei to call her Chanel. Auntie Mei, however, called every mother Baby's Ma, and every infant Baby. It was simple that way, one set of clients easily replaced by the next.

'It's not for you to like,' Auntie Mei said. The soup had simmered all morning and had thickened to a milky white. She would never have touched it herself, but it was the best recipe for breast-feeding mothers. 'You eat it for Baby.'

'Why do I have to eat for him?' Chanel said. She was skinny, though it had been only five days since the delivery.

'Why, indeed,' Auntie Mei said, laughing. 'Where else do you think your milk comes from?'

'I'm not a cow.'

I would rather you were a cow, Auntie Mei thought. But she merely threatened gently that there was always the option of formula. Auntie Mei wouldn't mind that, but most people hired her for her expertise in taking care of newborns and breast-feeding mothers.

The young woman started to sob. Really, Auntie Mei thought, she had never seen anyone so unfit to be a mother as this little creature.

'I think I have postpartum depression,' Chanel said when her tears had stopped.

Some fancy term the young woman had picked up.

'My great-grandmother hanged herself when my grandfather was three days old. People said she'd fallen under the spell of some passing ghost, but this is what I think.' Using her iPhone as a mirror, Chanel checked her face and pressed her puffy eyelids with a finger. 'She had postpartum depression.'

Auntie Mei stopped rocking and snuggled the infant closer. At once his head started bumping against her bosom. 'Don't speak nonsense,' she said sternly.

'I'm only explaining what postpartum depression is.'

'Your problem is that you're not eating. Nobody would be happy if they were in your shoes.'

'Nobody,' Chanel said glumly, 'could possibly be in my shoes. Do you know what I dreamt last night?'

'No.'

'Take a guess.'

'In our village, we say it's bad luck to guess someone else's dreams,' Auntie Mei said. Only ghosts entered and left people's minds freely.

'I dreamt that I flushed Baby down the toilet.'

'Oh. I wouldn't have guessed that even if I'd tried.'

'That's the problem. Nobody knows how I feel,' Chanel said, and started to weep again.

Auntie Mei sniffed under the child's blanket, paying no heed to the fresh tears. 'Baby needs a diaper change,' she announced, knowing that, given some time, Chanel would acquiesce: a mother is a mother, even if she speaks of flushing her child down the drain.

Auntie Mei had worked as a live-in nanny for newborns and their mothers for eleven years. As a rule, she moved out of the family's house the day a baby turned a month old, unless – though this rarely happened – she was between jobs, which was never more than a few days. Many families would have been glad to pay her extra for another week, or another month; some even offered a longer term, but Auntie

Mei always declined: she worked as a first-month nanny, whose duties, toward both the mother and the infant, were different from those of a regular nanny. Once in a while, she was approached by previous employers to care for their second child. The thought of facing a child who had once been an infant in her arms led to lost sleep; she agreed only when there was no other option, and she treated the older children as though they were empty air.

Between bouts of sobbing, Chanel said she did not understand why her husband couldn't take a few days off. The previous day he had left for Shenzhen on a business trip. 'What right does he have to leave me alone with his son?'

Alone? Auntie Mei squinted at Baby's eyebrows, knitted so tight that the skin in between took on a tinge of yellow. Your pa is working hard so your ma can stay home and call me nobody. The Year of the Snake, an inauspicious one to give birth in, had been slow for Auntie Mei; otherwise, she would've had better options. She had not liked the couple when she met them; unlike most expectant parents, they had both looked distracted, and asked few questions before offering her the position. They were about to entrust their baby to a stranger, Auntie Mei had wanted to remind them, but neither seemed worried. Perhaps they had gathered enough references? Auntie Mei did have a reputation as a gold-medal nanny. Her employers were the lucky ones, to have had a good education in China and, later, America, and to have become professionals in the Bay Area: lawyers, doctors, VCs, engineers – no matter, they still needed an experienced Chinese nanny for their American-born babies. Many families lined her up months before their babies were born.

Baby, cleaned and swaddled, seemed satisfied, so Auntie Mei left him on the changing table and looked out the window, enjoying, as she always did, a view that did not belong to her. Between an azalea bush and a slate path, there was a man-made pond, which hosted an assortment of goldfish and lily pads. Before he left, the husband had asked Auntie Mei to feed the fish and refill the pond. Eighteen hundred gallons a year, he had informed her, calculating the expense. She would have refused the additional responsibilities if not for his readiness to pay her an extra $20 each day.

A statue of an egret, balanced on one leg, stood in the water, its neck curved into a question mark. Auntie Mei thought about the man who had made the sculpture. Of course, it could have been a woman, but Auntie Mei refused to accept that possibility. She liked to believe that it was men who made beautiful and useless things like the egret. Let him be a lonely man, beyond the reach of any fiendish woman.

Baby started to wiggle. Don't you stir before your ma finishes her soup, Auntie Mei warned in a whisper, though in vain. The egret, startled, took off with an unhurried elegance, its single squawk stunning Auntie Mei and then making her laugh. For sure, you're getting old and forgetful: there was no such statue yesterday. Auntie Mei picked up Baby and went into the yard. There were fewer goldfish now, but at least some had escaped the egret's raid. All the same, she would have to tell Chanel about the loss. You think you have a problem with postpartum depression? Think of the goldfish, living one day in a paradise pond and the next day going to Heaven in the stomach of a passing egret.

Auntie Mei believed in strict routines for every baby and mother in her charge. For the first week, she fed the mother six meals a day, with three snacks in between; from the second week on, it was four meals and two snacks. The baby was to be nursed every two hours during the day, and every three or four hours at night. She let the parents decide whether the crib was kept in their bedroom or in the nursery, but she would not allow it in her bedroom. No, this was not for her convenience, she explained to them; there was simply no reason for a baby to be close to someone who was there for only a month.

'But it's impossible to eat so much. People are different,' Chanel said the next day. Less weepy at the moment, she was curled up on the sofa, a pair of heating pads on her chest: Auntie Mei had not been impressed with the young woman's milk production.

You can be as different as you want after I leave, Auntie Mei thought as she bathed Baby; your son can grow into a lopsided squash and I won't care a bit. But no mother or baby could deviate just yet. The reason people hired a first-month nanny, Auntie Mei told Chanel, was to make sure that things went correctly, not differently.

'But did you follow this schedule when you had your children? I bet you didn't.'

'As a matter of fact, I didn't, only because I didn't have children.'

'Not even one?'

'You didn't specify a nanny who had her own children.'

'But why would you ... why did you choose this line of work?'

Why indeed. 'Sometimes a job chooses you,' Auntie Mei said. Ha, who knew she could be so profound?

'But you must love children, then?'

Oh, no, no, not this one or that one; not any of them. 'Does a bricklayer love his bricks?'

15

Auntie Mei asked. 'Does the dishwasher repair-man love the dishwashers?' That morning, a man had come to look at Chanel's malfunction-ing dishwasher. It had taken him only twenty minutes of poking, but the bill was $100, as much as a whole day's wages for Auntie Mei.

'Auntie, that's not a good argument.'

'My job doesn't require me to argue well. If I could argue, I'd have become a lawyer, like your husband, no?'

Chanel made a mirthless laughing sound. Despite her self-diagnosed depression, she seemed to enjoy talking with Auntie Mei more than most mothers, who talked to her about their babies and their breast-feeding but otherwise had little interest in her.

Auntie Mei put Baby on the sofa next to Chanel, who was unwilling to make room.

'Now, let's look into this milk situation,' Auntie Mei said, rubbing her hands until they were warm before removing the heating pads. Chanel cried out in pain.

'I haven't even touched you.'

Look at your eyes, Auntie Mei wanted to say. Not even a good plumber could fix such a leak.

'I don't want to nurse this thing any more,' Chanel said.

This thing? 'He's your son.'

'His father's, too. Why can't he be here to help?'

'Men don't make milk.'

Chanel laughed, despite her tears. 'No. The only thing they make is money.'

'You're lucky to have found one who makes money. Not all of them do, you know.'

17

Chanel dried her eyes carefully with the inside of her pyjama sleeve. 'Auntie, are you married?'

'Once,' Auntie Mei said.

'What happened? Did you divorce him?'

'He died,' Auntie Mei said. She had, every day of her marriage, wished that her husband would stop being part of her life, though not in so absolute a manner. Now, years later, she still felt responsible for his death, as though it were she, and not a group of teenagers, who had accosted him that night. Why didn't you just let them take the money? Sometimes Auntie Mei scolded him when she tired of talking to herself. Thirty-five dollars for a life, three months short of fifty-two.

'Was he much older than you?'

'Older, yes, but not too old.'

'My husband is twenty-eight years older than I am,' Chanel said. 'I bet you didn't guess that.'

'No, I didn't.'

'Is it that I look old or that he looks young?'

'You look like a good match.'

'Still, he'll probably die before me, right? Women live longer than men, and he's had a head start.'

So you, too, are eager to be freed. Let me tell you, it's bad enough when a wish like that doesn't come true, but, if it ever does, that's when you know that living is a most disappointing business: the world is not a bright place to start with, but a senseless wish granted senselessly makes it much dimmer. 'Don't speak nonsense,' Auntie Mei said.

'I'm only stating the truth. How did your husband die? Was it a heart attack?'

'You could say that,' Auntie Mei said, and before Chanel could ask more questions Auntie Mei grabbed one of her erring breasts. Chanel gasped and then screamed. Auntie Mei did not let go until she'd given the breast a forceful massage. When she reached for the other breast, Chanel screamed louder but did not change her position, for fear of crushing Baby, perhaps.

Afterwards, Auntie Mei brought a warm towel. 'Go,' Chanel said. 'I don't want you here any more.'

'But who'll take care of you?'

'I don't need anyone to take care of me.' Chanel stood up and belted her robe.

'And Baby?'

'Bad luck for him.'

Chanel walked to the staircase, her back defiantly rigid. Auntie Mei picked up Baby, his weight as insignificant as the emotions – sadness, anger, or dismay – that she should feel on his behalf. Rather, Auntie Mei was in awe of the young woman. That is how, Auntie Mei said to herself, a mother orphans a child.

Baby, six days old that day, was weaned from his mother's breast. Auntie Mei was now the sole person to provide him with food and care and – this she did not want to admit even to herself – love. Chanel stayed in her bedroom and watched Chinese television dramas all afternoon. Once in a while, she came downstairs for water, and spoke to Auntie Mei as though the old woman and the infant were poor relations: there was the inconvenience of having them to stay, and yet there was relief that they did not have to be entertained.

The dishwasher repairman returned in the evening. He reminded Auntie Mei that his name was Paul. As though she were so old that she could forget it in a day, she thought. Earlier, she had told him about the thieving egret, and he had promised to come back and fix the problem.

'You're sure the bird won't be killed,' Auntie Mei said as she watched Paul rig some wires above the pond.

'Try it yourself,' Paul said, flipping the battery switch.

Auntie Mei placed her palm on the crisscrossed wires. 'I feel nothing.'

'Good. If you felt something, I'd be putting your life at risk. Then you could sue me.'

'But how does it work?'

'Let's hope the egret is more sensitive than you are,' Paul said. 'Call me if it doesn't work. I won't charge you again.'

Auntie Mei felt doubtful, but her questioning silence did not stop him from admiring his own invention. Nothing, he said, is too difficult for a thinking man. When he put away his tools he lingered on, and she could see that there was no reason for him to hurry home. He had grown up in Vietnam, he told Auntie Mei, and had come to America thirty-seven years ago. He was widowed, with three grown children, and none of them had given him a grandchild, or the hope of one. His two sisters, both living in New York and both younger, had beaten him at becoming grandparents.

The same old story: they all had to come from somewhere, and they all accumulated people along the way. Auntie Mei could see the unfolding of Paul's life: he'd work his days away till he was too old to be useful, then his children would deposit him in a facility and visit on his birthday and on holidays. Auntie Mei, herself an untethered woman, felt superior to him. She raised Baby's tiny fist as Paul was leaving. 'Say bye-bye to Grandpa Paul.'

Auntie Mei turned and looked up at the house. Chanel was leaning on the windowsill of her second-floor bedroom. 'Is he going to electrocute the egret?' she called down.

'He said it would only zap the bird. To teach it a lesson.'

'You know what I hate about people? They like to say, "That will teach you a lesson." But what's the point of a lesson? There's no make-up exam when you fail something in life.'

It was October, and the evening air from the Bay had a chill to it. Auntie Mei had nothing to say except to warn Chanel not to catch a cold.

'Who cares?'

'Maybe your parents do.'

Chanel made a dismissive noise.

'Or your husband.'

'Ha. He just emailed and told me he had to stay for another ten days,' Chanel said. 'You know what I think he's doing right now? Sleeping with a woman, or more than one.'

Auntie Mei did not reply. It was her policy not to disparage an employer behind his back. But when she entered the house Chanel was already in the living room. 'I think you should know he's not the kind of person you thought he was.'

'I don't think he's any kind of person at all,' Auntie Mei said.

'You never say a bad word about him,' Chanel said.

Not a good word, either.

'He had a wife and two children before.'

You think a man, any man, would remain a bachelor until he meets you? Auntie Mei put the slip of paper with Paul's number in her pocket.

'Did that man leave you his number?' Chanel said. 'Is he courting you?'

'Him? Half of him, if not more, is already in the coffin.'

'Men chase after women until the last moment,' Chanel said. 'Auntie, don't fall for him. No man is to be trusted.'

Auntie Mei sighed. 'If Baby's Pa is not coming home, who's going to shop for groceries?'

The man of the house postponed his return; Chanel refused to have anything to do with Baby. Against her rules, Auntie Mei moved his crib into her bedroom; against her rules, too, she took on the responsibility of grocery shopping.

'Do you suppose people will think we're

the grandparents of this baby?' Paul asked after inching the car into a tight spot between two SUVs.

Could it be that he had agreed to drive and help with shopping for a reason other than the money Auntie Mei had promised him? 'Nobody,' she said, handing a list to Paul, 'will think anything. Baby and I will wait here in the car.'

'You're not coming in?'

'He's a brand-new baby. You think I would bring him into a store with a bunch of refrigerators?'

'You should've left him home, then.'

With whom? Auntie Mei worried that, had she left Baby home, he would be gone from the world when she returned, though this fear she would not share with Paul. She explained that Baby's Ma suffered from post-partum depression and was in no shape to take care of him.

'You should've just given me the shopping list,' Paul said.

What if you ran off with the money without delivering the groceries, she thought, though it was unfair of her. There were men she knew she could trust, including, even, her dead husband.

On the drive back, Paul asked if the egret had returned. She hadn't noticed, Auntie Mei replied. She wondered if she would have an opportunity to see the bird be taught its lesson: she had only twenty-two days left. Twenty-two days, and then the next family would pluck her out of here, egret or no egret. Auntie Mei turned to look at Baby, who was asleep in the car seat. 'What will become of you then?' she said.

'Me?' Paul asked.

'Not you. Baby.'

'Why do you worry? He'll have a good life. Better than mine. Better than yours, for sure.'

'You don't know my life to say that,' Auntie Mei said.

'I can imagine. You should find someone. This is not a good life for you, going from one house to another and never settling down.'

'What's wrong with that? I don't pay rent. I don't have to buy my own food.'

'What's the point of making money if you don't spend it?' Paul said. 'I'm at least saving money for my future grandchildren.'

'What I do with my money,' Auntie Mei said, 'is none of your business. Now, please pay attention to the road.'

Paul, chastened into a rare silence, drove on, the slowest car on the freeway. Perhaps he'd meant well, but there were plenty of well-meaning men, and she was one of those women who made such men suffer. If Paul wanted to hear stories, she could tell him one or two, and spare him any hope of winning her affection. But where would she start? With the man she had married without any intention of loving and had wished into an early grave, or with the father she had not met because her mother had made his absolute absence a condition of her birth? Or perhaps she should start with her grandmother, who vanished from her own daughter's cribside

31

one day, only to show up twenty-five years later when her husband was dying from a wasting illness. The disappearance would have made sense had Auntie Mei's grandfather been a villain, but he had been a kind man, and had raised his daughter alone, clinging to the hope that his wife, having left without a word, would return.

Auntie Mei's grandmother had not gone far: all those years, she had stayed in the same village, living with another man, hiding in his attic during the day, sneaking out of the house in the middle of the night for a change of air. Nobody was able to understand why she had not gone on hiding until after her husband's death. She explained that it was her wifely duty to see her husband off properly. Auntie Mei's mother, newly married and with a prospering business as a seamstress, was said to have accepted one parent's return and the other's death with equanimity, but the next year, pregnant with her first and only child, she made her husband leave by threatening to drink a bottle of DDT.

Auntie Mei had been raised by two mythic women. The villagers had shunned the two women, but they had welcomed the girl as one of them. Behind closed doors, they had told her about her grandfather and her father, and in their eyes she had seen their fearful disapproval of her elders: her pale-skinned grandmother, unused to daylight after years of darkness, had carried on her nocturnal habits, cooking and knitting for her daughter and granddaughter in the middle of the night; her mother, eating barely enough, had slowly starved herself to death, yet she never tired of watching, with an unblinking intensity, her daughter eat.

Auntie Mei had not thought of leaving home until the two women died, her mother first, and then her grandmother. They had been sheltered from worldly reproach by their peculiarities when alive; in death, they took with them their habitat, and left nothing to anchor Auntie Mei. A marriage offer, arranged by the distant cousin of a man in Queens, New York, had been accepted without hesitation: in a new country, her grandmother and her mother would cease to be legendary. Auntie Mei had not told her husband about them; he would not have been interested, in any case – silly good man, wanting only a hard-working woman to share a solid life. Auntie Mei turned to look at Paul. Perhaps he was not so different from her husband, her father, her grandfather, or even the man her grandmother had lived with for years but never returned to after the death of Auntie Mei's grandfather: ordinary happiness, uncomplicated by the women in their lives, was their due.

'You think, by any chance, you'll be free tomorrow afternoon?' Paul asked when he'd parked the car in front of Chanel's house.

'I work all day, as you know.'

'You could bring Baby, like you did today.'

'To where?'

Paul said that there was this man who played chess every Sunday afternoon at East-West Plaza Park. Paul wanted to take a walk with Auntie Mei and Baby nearby.

Auntie Mei laughed. 'Why, so he'll get distracted and lose the game?'

'I want him to think I've done better than him.'

Better how? With a borrowed lady friend pushing a borrowed grandson in a stroller? 'Who is he?'

'Nobody important. I haven't talked to him for twenty-seven years.'

He couldn't even lie well. 'And you still think he'd fall for your trick?'

'I know him.'

Auntie Mei wondered if knowing someone – a friend, an enemy – was like never letting that person out of one's sight. Being known, then, must not be far from being imprisoned by someone else's thought. In that sense, her grandmother and her mother had been fortunate: no one could claim to have known them, not even Auntie Mei. When she was younger, she had seen no point in understanding them, as she had been told they were beyond apprehension. After their deaths, they had become abstract. Not knowing them, Auntie Mei, too, had the good fortune of not wanting to know anyone who came after: her husband; her co-workers at various Chinese restaurants during her year-long migration from New York to San Francisco; the babies and the mothers she took care of, who had become only recorded names in her notebook. 'I'd say let it go,' Auntie Mei told Paul. 'What kind of grudge is worthy of twenty-seven years?'

Paul sighed. 'If I tell you the story, you'll understand.'

'Please,' Auntie Mei said. 'Don't tell me any story.'

From the second-floor landing, Chanel watched Paul put the groceries in the refrigerator and Auntie Mei warm up a bottle of formula. Only after he'd left did Chanel call down to ask how their date had gone. Auntie Mei held Baby in the rocking chair; the joy of watching him eat was enough of a compensation for his mother's being a nuisance.

Chanel came downstairs and sat on the sofa. 'I saw you pull up. You stayed in the car for a long time,' she said. 'I didn't know an old man could be so romantic.'

Auntie Mei thought of taking Baby into her bedroom, but this was not her house, and she knew that Chanel, in a mood to talk, would follow her. When Auntie Mei remained quiet, Chanel said that her husband had called earlier, and she had told him that his son had gone out to witness a couple carry on a sunset affair.

You should walk out right this minute, Auntie Mei said to herself, but her body settled into the rhythm of the rocking chair, back and forth, back and forth.

'Are you angry, Auntie?'

'What did your husband say?'

'He was upset, of course, and I told him that's what he gets for not coming home.'

What's stopping you from leaving, Auntie Mei asked herself. You want to believe you're staying for Baby, don't you?

'You should be happy for me that he's upset,' Chanel said. 'Or at least happy for Baby, no?'

I'm happy that, like everyone else, you'll all become the past soon.

'Why are you so quiet, Auntie? I'm sorry I'm such a pain, but I don't have a friend here, and you've been nice to me. Would you please take care of me and Baby?'

'You're paying me,' Auntie Mei said. 'So of course I'll take care of you.'

'Will you be able to stay on after this month?' Chanel asked. 'I'll pay double.'

'I don't work as a regular nanny.'

'But what would we do without you, Auntie?'

Don't let this young woman's sweet voice deceive you, Auntie Mei warned herself: you're not irreplaceable – not for her, not for Baby, not for anyone. Still, Auntie Mei fancied for a moment that she could watch

Baby grow – a few months, a year, two years. 'When is Baby's Pa coming home?'

'He'll come home when he comes.'

Auntie Mei cleaned Baby's face with the corner of a towel.

'I know what you're thinking – that I didn't choose the right man. Do you want to know how I came to marry someone so old and irresponsible?'

'I don't, as a matter of fact.'

All the same, they told Auntie Mei stories, not heeding her protests. The man who played chess every Sunday afternoon came from the same village as Paul's wife, and had long ago been pointed out to him by her as a potentially better husband. Perhaps she had said it only once, out of an impulse to sting

Paul, or perhaps she had tormented him for years with her approval of a former suitor. Paul did not say, and Auntie Mei did not ask. Instead, he had measured his career against the man's: Paul had become a real professional; the man had stayed a labourer.

An enemy could be as eternally close as a friend; a feud could make two men brothers for life. Fortunate are those for whom everyone can be turned into a stranger, Auntie Mei thought, but this wisdom she did not share with Paul. He had wanted her only to listen, and she had obliged him.

Chanel, giving more details, and making Auntie Mei blush at times, was a better storyteller. She had slept with an older married man to punish her father, who had himself pursued a young woman, in this case one of

Chanel's college classmates. The pregnancy was meant to punish her father, too, but also the man, who, like her father, had cheated on his wife. 'He didn't know who I was at first. I made up a story so that he thought I was one of those girls he could sleep with and then pay off,' Chanel had said. 'But then he realised he had no choice but to marry me. My father has enough connections to destroy his business.'

Had she not thought how this would make her mother feel? Auntie Mei asked. Why should she? Chanel replied. A woman who could not keep the heart of her man was not a good model for a daughter.

Auntie Mei did not understand their logic: Chanel's depraved; Paul's unbending. What a world you've been born into, Auntie Mei said to Baby now. It was past midnight, the lamp in her bedroom turned off. The night-light of swimming ocean animals on the crib streaked Baby's face blue and orange. There must have been a time when her mother had sat with her by candlelight, or else her grandmother might have been there in the darkness. What kind of future had they wished for her? She had been brought up in two worlds: the world of her grandmother and her mother, and that of everyone else; each world had sheltered her from the other, and to lose one was to be turned, against her wish, into a permanent resident of the other.

Auntie Mei came from a line of women who could not understand themselves, and in not knowing themselves they had derailed their men and orphaned their children. At least Auntie Mei had had the sense not to have a child, though sometimes, during a sleepless night like this one, she entertained the thought of slipping away with a baby she could love. The world was vast; there had to be a place for a woman to raise a child as she wished.

The babies – 131 of them, and their parents, trusting yet vigilant – had protected Auntie Mei from herself. But who was going to protect her now? Not this baby, who was as defenceless as the others, yet she must protect him. From whom, though: his parents, who had no place for him in their hearts, or Auntie Mei, who had begun to imagine his life beyond the one month allocated to her?

See, this is what you get for sitting up and muddling your head. Soon you'll become a tiresome oldster like Paul, or a lonely woman like Chanel, telling stories to any available ear. You can go on talking and thinking about your mother and your grandmother and all those women before them, but the problem is, you don't know them. If knowing some-one makes that person stay with you forever, not knowing someone does the same trick: death does not take the dead away; it only makes them grow more deeply into you.

No one would be able to stop her if she picked up Baby and walked out the door. She could turn herself into her grandmother, for whom sleep had become optional in the end; she could turn herself into her mother, too, eating little because it was Baby who needed nourishment. She could become a fugitive from this world that had kept her for too long, but this urge, coming as it often did in waves, no longer frightened her, as it had years ago. She was getting older, more forgetful, yet she was also closer to comprehending the danger of being herself. She had, unlike her mother and her grandmother, talked herself into being a woman with an ordinary fate. When she moved on to the next place, she would leave no mystery or damage behind; no one in this world would be disturbed by having known her.

About the Author

Yiyun Li grew up in Beijing and came to the United States in 1996. Her debut collection, *A Thousand Years of Good Prayers*, won the Frank O'Connor International Short Story Award and the *Guardian* First Book Award. Her novel, *The Vagrants*, was shortlisted for the Dublin IMPAC Award. Her books have been translated into more than twenty languages. She was selected by *Granta* as one of the 21 Best Young American Novelists under 35, and was named by *The New Yorker* as one of the top 20 writers under 40. She lives in Oakland, California with her husband and their two sons.